Young Readers' Series

On the Trail of the
GRIZZLY

Carol A. Amato
Illustrated by Patrick O'Brien

BARRON'S

Acknowledgments

Many thanks to Willie Karidis, executive director of the Denali Foundation in Denali Park, Alaska, for his help and encouragement.

Special thanks to Warren Bratter, project editor for the Young Readers' Series, who worked diligently with me; ours was a collaboration of the mind and heart as we inspired one another so that our young readers will learn to care passionately, as we do.

This book is dedicated to Phil, Maria, and Nicole who share, with love, my sense of wonder.

Text © Copyright 1997 by Carol A. Amato
Illustrations © Copyright 1997 by Patrick O'Brien

All inquiries should be addressed to:
Barron's Educational Series, Inc.
250 Wireless Boulevard
Hauppauge, New York 11788

International Standard Book No. 0-8120-9312-7

Library of Congress Catalog Card No. 96-19930
Library of Congress Cataloging-in-Publication Data
Amato, Carol A.
     On the trail of the grizzly / by Carol A. Amato ; illustrated by
Patrick O'Brien
          p. cm.—(Young readers' series)
     Summary: While visiting their grandmother in Alaska, Kate and David encounter
a grizzly and make discoveries about that animal and its disappearing habitat.
          ISBN 0-8120-9312-7
          [1. Grizzly bear—Fiction.   2. Bears—Fiction.   3. Alaska—Fiction
4. Endangered species—Fiction.   5. Grandmothers—Fiction.]
I. O'Brien, Patrick, 1960–   ill. II. Title.   III. Series: Amato, Carol A.   Young readers' series.
     PZ7.A49160n   1997
     [Fic]—dc20   96-19930
                                                                                  CIP
                                                                                  AC

PRINTED IN HONG KONG
987654321

Table of Contents

"David! Kate!" Gram called. "Will you please go out to the woodpile and bring in some wood?"

"Sure, Gram," they both answered. The children put on their coats and boots and walked out to the woodpile behind the cabin.

"Bet I can carry more than you!" said David.

"Bet you can't!" replied Kate.

They both filled their arms with wood. Kate finished first and raced back ahead of David. Suddenly, David heard Kate scream. When he reached her, a huge brown bear was standing on its hind legs right in front of her. Two little bears were right behind it. The children both dropped their wood and just stared at the bear with their mouths open. Then David remembered what Gram had told them.

"Play dead," he whispered to Kate. Slowly, they both lay face down in the snow. They barely breathed. The big bear stooped down and sniffed them. Then it turned around and began walking toward the woods with the little ones running behind. When the bears were out of sight, the children got up and ran into the cabin.

"Gram! Gram!" Kate shouted. "Some bears almost ate us!"

"But we played dead," said David.

Gram hurried to the door and opened it. She watched the bears as they disappeared into the woods.

"Good for you, kids," she said. "You were lucky. The bear did not sense that you would harm her or her

4

cubs, so she did not attack. I know that bear—she ate most of my blueberries last summer. By the size of them, I'd say her cubs are about three months old."

"Why are they here now, Gram?" asked David.

"They may be looking for food," answered Gram. "Some of the bears around here are used to people."

"I thought bears were wild animals," said
Kate.

Gram got that storytelling look on her face.

"Long ago," she began, "your grandpa and I built this
cabin in Alaska. There was and still is a national park
not far from here."

"Does it have swings and slides?" asked David.

"Not *that* kind of park," laughed Gram. "National
parks were made to protect wildlife. They were also
made so that people could visit the park to enjoy the
beautiful wilderness."

"But why did the bears get used to people?" asked Kate.

"I'm about to tell you" said Gram. "When people came to the park, they saw bears and other wild animals. Some people fed them, and some left food in their campsites. Food was also piled in the park's dumps. Once the bears tasted people-food, they couldn't get enough of it. If people are near the food, the bears can be dangerous."

"Would they attack the people in the park?" asked Kate.

"A while ago, a few bears did attack people in the park. Most bears attack because people surprise them, and the bears think they are in danger. Others destroyed campgrounds looking for food. Some of these bears were captured and moved far away. Many of them still found their way back to the park. A few were killed because they were thought to be dangerous."

"It doesn't seem fair to the bears," said Kate.

"It wasn't," said Gram. "The park bears had lived on the park land long before people came. People caused

them to change the way they lived in the wild. Now, at last, there are many rules to try to keep bears and people apart. There are no more dumps. Food must be kept in special containers so the smell won't attract bears. People can camp in the park, but they must stay far away from the animals. They can see wildlife from buses that take them through the park."

"Gram, why wasn't the father bear with them?" asked Kate.

"That's a good question, Kate," said Gram.

"Here comes another story!" David whispered to Kate.

"*As* I was saying," Gram continued, "the male (or boy) and the female (or girl) bears mate in the summer so they can have babies. But the male doesn't stay with

the female for long. After the cubs are born, only the mother takes care of them."

"That's kind of like our family," said David, "except that our dad died. Now only Mom takes care of us."

"And you, too, Gram," said Kate, "when Mom has to go away on a trip for her job."

"Yes," said Gram, "and like the bears, we are *still* a family. After all, what makes a family is love and caring, whoever takes care of you."

The next morning, Gram woke the children early.

"How would you like to go snowshoe hiking?" Gram asked.

"Wow!" they said together.

"I guess that means yes!" said Gram.

"What if we surprise a bear?" asked Kate. "Will it attack us?"

"We will be in open country, on the tundra," answered Gram. "We may see the bears in the distance, but we will never hike near them."

"You know, Gramps and I spent many years learning about the grizzlies. They are also called big brown bears. We never put ourselves in danger by getting too close to them. We respected their wildness. The three of us will, too."

Gram showed the children
how to walk in the snowshoes.
It was harder than it looked.
After some practice, Gram
said, "Let's go!"
Gram and the children
hiked along the open tundra.
They came to a river. The spring sun
had melted bare spots on it.
"Look, kids, there's a snowshoe hare," said Gram.
"Where are its snowshoes?" asked David.
Gram laughed. "Its feet are so long, they're as good
as snowshoes!"

Kate walked ahead of the others, then stopped.

"Gram and David!" she called. "I see the bears! Look, way out there. The chocolate cub is rolling down a hill."

Soon both of the cubs were tumbling down. A pile of snow fell on top of the straw-colored cub. She looked so surprised! Even the mother bear joined in the snowslide.

"This is fun to watch," said Gram. "The mother doesn't often join in the cubs' play."

"Why not?" asked David.

"She is a strict teacher," answered Gram. "The cubs will not be safe unless they learn to obey her at all times."

The mother bear shook the snow from her fur. She "woofed" softly. The cubs stopped sliding right away. Then she stood on her short hind legs, her nose pointing into the breeze.

"She may have our scent, or smell," said Gram. "We'd better head back. Bears can sense danger from far away."

After they had gone a short way, Gram stopped walking.

"Look, children," she said. "There's a hole under that hill. It might be a bear den."

"Let's get out of here," said Kate. "The bears might come back!"

"If they do, we'll call you Katie-locks," laughed her brother. "Then you can run away from the three bears' house just like *she* did!"

"Don't worry," said Gram. "The bears use their dens only in winter. In the warmer months, they gather branches of pine and spruce trees to sleep on."

Gram bent down and looked inside the den. At the end of the tunnel was a bigger space, with a large pile of dried grass and small tree branches.

"Look, children," she said, as she moved away from the small den opening. They took turns looking inside.

"Awesome!" Kate and David said at the same time.

"Do bears always dig their own dens?" asked David.

"Not always," said Gram. "Sometimes they find a cave or a big hollow tree. Bears are fussy about their dens. The den must be both safe and warm."

"It does look kind of cozy in there," said Kate.

"Why don't you go inside and fall asleep in the baby bear's bed, Katie-locks!" laughed David.

"Very funny," said Kate. "Gram, we learned in school that bears hibernate."

"That's right, Kate," said Gram, "but the bear's

hibernation is different from that of other hibernating animals."

"In what way?" asked David.

"Animals like woodchucks fall into a light sleep. They wake up to eat and drink. Bears sleep deeply. For as long as seven months, they do not eat or drink. They lose a lot of fat, so they must eat a lot before they hibernate in the fall. All winter, they live off this fat. When they leave their dens in the spring, they are soon hungry."

"We must be going," said Gram. "I'll bet you're getting hungry, too!"

Chapter 3 The Camping Trip

Soon the spring snow melted. The land seemed to turn green overnight. Only the high mountains still had snow that would never melt.

Kate and David played happily during the long summer days. On hikes with Gram, they saw animals they had never seen before.

One day during lunch, Gram said to the children, "I have a surprise for you. We're going camping!"

"Hooray!" David and Kate shouted.

"We may be near a part of the grizzly's home range," said Gram. "To be safe, we'll stay in a cabin that no longer belongs to anyone."

"What's a home range?" asked Kate.

"An animal's home range is the space it needs and uses to hunt and raise its young," answered Gram. "The grizzly's home range may be just a few miles or hundreds of miles. It will stay in this home range for the twenty to thirty years that it lives."

"Where else do grizzlies live besides Alaska, Gram?" asked Kate. "Around the world, they may live in forests, swamplands, prairies, and deserts. All the grizzly needs is to be left alone in a place big enough for it to find food and raise its young," Gram answered.

Early the next morning, they were packed and ready to go. They began to hike, following the bend of the river. They saw caribou and their young calves crossing a narrow part of the river.

"Last year there was a wolf den near here," said Gram. "I think—"

As she spoke, David said, "Look! Down by the river bend. Wolves! And they're surrounding a bear and her cubs!"

"Those are our grizzlies," said Gram. "I can see a dead animal near them. It may be a caribou calf. The bears or the wolves probably killed it, but both of these hunters want this meal."

"How sad," said Kate. "Why did they kill a little calf, Gram?"

"I know that it seems mean, but it's really not," said Gram. "Bears and wolves are predators. They must kill to eat and live. Remember, many people also eat the meat of animals. We do not have to hunt them, but they are killed and sold in our markets."

The grizzly was ready to attack. She lowered her head to the ground and stared into the wolves' eyes. They stared back. The bear popped her jaws together loudly. Suddenly, the straw-colored cub moved away from her. Two of the wolves moved toward it. The mother bear "woofed" sharply. The cub obeyed and ran under her belly.

"GRRrr! Woof!" Don't get too close, she warned, standing on her hind legs.

That was enough for the wolves. They fled in fear. The mother bear began eating the dead calf while the cubs watched.

"That was scary!" said David. "Why aren't the cubs eating, too, Gram?"

"They're still nursing," said Gram. "Bear cubs drink their mother's milk until they are about two and a half years old. Soon after that, they're ready to take care of themselves."

Chapter 4: The Grizzly Grizzlies

The mother bear stood on her hind legs. She looked and listened carefully. Then she walked a few steps and sniffed the breeze. She sensed that the danger had passed. She began to walk fast, and then broke into a run. The cubs tried to catch up with her.

"Look at her go!" said Kate.

"Grizzlies are fast," said Gram. "They can run about 35 miles (56 kilometers) an hour. They can also travel all day and all night without resting."

"It looks like the mother was in a big hurry to get to those berry bushes," said Gram. "She can smell berries from very far away!"

The cubs began to chase one another. They rolled around in the wildflowers and wrestled with each other. They bit and boxed.

"Those cubs are having so much fun!" said David.

"You children are all alike," Gram laughed, "but some of the bear cubs' play helps them get ready for being grown-up bears."

"Gram, why is there a big hump on the grizzly's shoulder?" asked Kate.

"That bump is a big muscle called a roach," said Gram. "It helps the bear to dig and to fight with its big front legs. You can see how huge she is. A grizzly can weigh more than 600 hundred pounds (270 kilograms).

The males are larger than the females."

"She even has a big head," said David. "It's kind of flat like a dish."

"Good observations, children!" said Gram. "If we were close enough, you could see her long claws. They are 4 to 6 inches (10.1 to 15.2 centimeters) long, and she can use them almost like fingers."

"But Gram, why is a grizzly *called* a grizzly?" asked Kate.

"Well," said Gram, "in summer, the bear's winter coat falls off in patches. Under this is a dark, new coat with silver-gray hairs. This coat makes the bear look shaggy. The word grizzly means 'streaked with gray'."

"Your hair looks kind of grizzly, too, Gram!" said David. They all laughed.

"We'd better find the cabin," said Gram.

They walked along the carpet of high tundra. Soon they came to a small ridge that stuck out from a hill.

"There's the cabin," said Gram.

Gram and the children went inside.

In Alaska, there is no true darkness in the summer. Each day, the sun shines for twenty hours. That night, Gram and the children slept in the cabin under the twilight sky. Lying in their sleeping bags, they listened to the howl of wolves. The sounds seemed near, then far away.

The next morning, they walked again along the dry tundra of the high ground. Suddenly, Gram stopped walking.

"Look, children," she said, pointing ahead. "The bears are grazing in that meadow."

"Grazing like cows do?" asked Kate.

"Well, somewhat like cows," laughed Gram. "Bears eat more long grass than anything else. They also eat all kinds of plants and roots. But their special love is berries—blueberries, bearberries, soapberries, huckleberries, cranberries, buffaloberries."

"Enough berries!" said Kate.

"But Gram," said David, "we saw the bear eating the caribou calf. That was meat."

Blueberries

Cranberries

Bearberries

Huckleberries

Buffaloberries

"That's right, David," said Gram. "Bears are omnivorous. That's a big word that means they eat both plants and meat. When a grizzly feeds on large, dead animals it rips the meat apart with its powerful jaws. This makes it possible for smaller animals like coyotes and ravens to eat the meat when the bear is done."

"Then we're omnivorous, too," said Kate. "We eat vegetables, which are plants, and meat."

"Yes," said Gram, "although some people don't eat meat."

"On TV, I saw grizzlies eating fish in a river," said David.

"They love to eat fish. Along the coast of Alaska, the grizzlies are larger and are wonderful fishermen," said Gram.

"Don't you mean 'fisher-bears'?" Kate said. They all laughed.

"Well, the 'fisher-bears' can't fish in this part of Alaska," said Gram.

"Huge glaciers of ice stir up the earth as they move in the sea. This fine earth goes into the rivers and streams. Fish cannot live in these waters."

"Gram, don't bears eat honey, like Winnie-the-Pooh?" asked David.

"Just like Winnie," said Gram, "and they don't even mind getting their noses stung to get it!"

"Look," said Kate, "the cubs seem to be chasing something."

"It may be a ground squirrel or even a grasshopper," said Gram. "The cubs are learning to hunt, but they may not catch much yet!"

The mother bear looked up from the blueberry patch to watch her playful cubs. Her snout was stained deep blue from the berries. Suddenly, she stood up on her hind legs and sniffed the air. In the distance, an enormous brown bear was running toward her and the cubs. He stopped running when he was a few feet away from them. He stared at the mother bear. She stared back. Then she looked back at her cubs.

"Rummpf," she said, softly. The chocolate cub quickly ran to her. The straw cub took too long. The big bear charged the cub. The mother bear ran toward him. Her anger made her powerful! She rose up on her hind legs and sprang forward. Her long, sharp claws dug into his nose.

"GRRrr!" he roared in pain, holding on to his bleeding nose. Then he turned and walked quickly away across the meadow.

The mother bear shook herself. She turned around and hit the straw cub with her great padded paw. The cub had not obeyed and almost lost her life.

"Awesome!" David and Kate said at the same time.

"Why did the big bear attack them, Gram?" asked David.

"That big bear was a male," said Gram. "Male bears will eat cubs if they can. That cub was lucky. Her mother saved its life. A mother bear will risk her own life to protect her cubs."

The afternoon air began to cool.

"It's getting late," said Gram. "We'd better head back to the cabin."

They watched as the mother bear began grazing again as if nothing had happened. The cubs chased butterflies.

"Good-bye, bears," said David.

"And stay near your mama!" warned Kate.

They walked through the fields of wild pea vine and colorful wildflowers. The low light cast purple shadows on the mountain that loomed more than 20,000 feet (6,096 meters) above them.

"When will the bears hibernate?" Kate asked her grandmother.

"In Alaska, grizzlies go into their dens around October," she answered. "If the mother has one- or two-year-old cubs, they will hibernate with her. They will snuggle up together to keep warm."

"But when and where are new cubs born?" asked David.

"Around January, the mother bear gives birth right in the winter den," said Gram. "A female bear without cubs may mate with a male in the summer. If the female is fat and healthy by winter, the egg inside her will begin to grow. If she is not healthy, the egg will not grow."

"That's amazing!" said Kate. "Are the cubs born while she's hibernating?" she asked.

"Yes," answered Gram. "The mother wakes to give birth to one, two, or sometimes even three cubs. The cubs begin nursing right away, even when the mother goes back to sleep. They weigh only about 1.5 pounds (0.67 kilograms) and are about the size of a small

squirrel. The tiny cubs are nearly furless and have no teeth."

"Do the cubs hibernate, too?" asked David.

"No," said Gram. "At about three weeks old, they crawl about the den. At six weeks old, their eyes open. They now have soft, silky hair and look just like teddy bears!"

"When will the bears leave the den, Gram?" asked Kate.

"Here in Alaska, bears leave their dens from late April and early May," said Gram. "The curious cubs are ready to explore their bright new world!"

When Gram and the children reached the cabin, the twilight sky was streaked with pink and gold. The children helped to prepare dinner. They rested beside the campfire outside and made yummy *s'mores*.

"Gram," said Kate, "why are you so quiet tonight?"

"Well," said Gram, "I've been thinking about the grizzlies. You know, bears are quite different from one another. No two bears behave in the same way. I have also seen bears look happy, sad, mad, worried, afraid, scared, and even guilty!"

"Like people-feelings?" asked David.

"Yes," said Gram, "but of course, bears and people are not the same in many other ways. In the early days, the Native Americans knew this. They both feared and respected the bear and other wild animals. In the old legend, it was the bear who taught people how to survive. Now only people can decide if bears and other animals will survive."

"Can we help decide?" said Kate.

"You can," said Gram. "Learn as much as you can about the living world around you. The earth is beautiful and amazing! Your learning will lead to love and caring. When you are older, you can help to make laws to protect wildlife. To do this, we must also protect the land, air, and water of the earth so that we *all* can survive. People must learn how to share the earth with other living things so we can *all* survive together."

In the distance, a lone wolf howled. Somewhere in the rolling hills, a mother bear slept peacefully with her cubs on a soft bed of pine.

Afterword

The Native American people respected the spirit of all animals. Even when an animal was hunted and killed, its spirit was honored with special events. The spirit of the bear was especially powerful. Bear teeth and claws were used as good-luck charms.

Many years ago, there were many bears and Native Americans everywhere. This would all end with the opening of the West in the early 1800s. Thousands of Indians were killed for their land. Thousands of grizzlies were killed for food, hides, and protection of ranchers' cattle and sheep. They were also killed simply because people were afraid of them. It is believed that 100,000 grizzlies once roamed the American West. Today there are fewer than 1,000. About 10,000 grizzlies still live in Alaska.

When people come, grizzlies are forced to go. Woods and meadows become farmland and cities. Before long, the bear's home ranges are no longer theirs.

In 1973, the Endangered Species Act listed the grizzly as threatened in the lower forty-eight states of the United States. This meant that the grizzly was in danger of disappearing in these places if they were not protected. Since that time, many groups have begun working to save the grizzly. In some places, like Yellowstone National Park, grizzlies are making a comeback. They have also been sighted in a few other northwestern states. In parks like Denali National Park in Alaska, new rules and regulations keep visitors away from bears so that the bears will return to their wild ways. With the help of concerned people and strict laws, the grizzly may once again be free to roam and search for berries in a vast, protected wilderness.

Glossary

Asia (A-sia) the largest continent, or land mass, of the Earth. It borders Europe.

bear species (SPE-cies) There are eight different kinds, or species, of bears: American black bear, Asiatic black bear, big brown bear, panda, polar bear, sloth bear, spectacled bear, and the sun bear.

beaver (BEA-ver) a rodent with webbed hind feet and a broad flat tail. Beavers make dams and underwater lodges, or homes.

caribou (CAR-i-bou) deer with large antlers that live in northern North America. They are related to the reindeer.

Dall sheep a large, white, wild sheep of northwestern North America.

desert (DES-ert) dry and sandy area of the world with little or no water.

Europe (EUR-ope) the continent between Asia and the Atlantic Ocean.

home range the territory that an animal or group of animals calls its own. A home range can be a short distance or cover more than 1,000 miles.

loon a fish-eating, diving bird that lives in northern parts of the world. Its calls and cries are eerie and can be heard for miles.

moose a large mammal in the deer family found in the forests of Canada and the northern United States.

omnivorous (om-NIV-or-ous) a word describing animals that eat both plants and meat (or fish). Herbivorous (her-BIV-or-ous) animals eat plants only. Carnivorous (car-NIV-or-ous) animals hunt and kill animals for food or eat dead animals they find.

prairie (PRAIR-ie) a large area of flat or rolling land with few trees.

roach (ROA-ch) a big muscle on the grizzly's shoulder. It looks like a big bump.

s'mores (s-MORES) a simple dessert for picnics and camping. To make s'mores, place half of a flat chocolate bar on one side of a graham cracker. Toast a marshmallow. Put the marshmallow on top of the chocolate. Put a second graham cracker on top of it all. Squeeze together gently. Eat. Yum. "Do you want *some more?*"

tundra (TUN-dra) the treeless plains in northern parts of the world. Tundra meadows are wet with black, mucky soil. The high-ground tundra is dry.

twilight (TWI-light) the time between sunset and full night.

Yellowstone National Park (YELL-o-stone NA-tion-al Park) a large wildlife park and preserve in parts of northwestern Wyoming, eastern Idaho and southern Montana.

Dear Parents and Educators:

Welcome to the Young Readers' series!

These learning stories have been created to introduce young children to the study of animals.

Children's earliest exposure to reading is usually through fiction. Stories read aloud invite children into the world of words and imagination. If children are read to frequently, this becomes a highly anticipated form of entertainment. Often that same pleasure is felt when children learn to read on their own. Nonfiction books are also read aloud to children but generally when they are older. However, interest in the "real" world emerges early in life, as soon as children develop a sense of wonder about everything around them.

There are a number of excellent read-aloud natural-science books available. Educators and parents agree that children love nonfiction books about animals. Unfortunately, there are very few that can be read *by* young children. One of the goals of the Young Readers' series is to happily fill that gap!

On the Trail of the Grizzly is one in a series of learning stories designed to appeal to young readers. In the classroom, the series can be incorporated into literature-based or whole-language programs, and would be especially suitable for science theme teaching units. Within planned units, each book may serve as a springboard to immersion techniques that include hands-on activities, field study trips, and additional research and reading. Many of the books are also concerned with the threatened or endangered status of the species studied and the role even young people can play in the preservation plan.

These books can also serve as read-aloud for young children. Weaving information through a story form lends itself easily to reading aloud. Hopefully, this book and others in the series will provide entertainment and wonder for both young readers and listeners.

C.A.

In the Classroom

One of the goals of this series is to introduce the young child to factual information related to the species being studied. The science terminology used is relevant to the learning process for the young student. In the classroom, you may want to use multi-modality methods to ensure understanding and word recognition. The following suggestions may be helpful:

1. Refer to the pictures when possible for difficult words and discuss how these words can be used in another context.
2. Encourage the children to use word and sentence contextual clues when approaching unknown words. They should be encouraged to use the glossary since it is an important information adjunct to the story.
3. After the children read the story or individual chapter, you may want to involve them in discussions using a variety of questioning techniques:

    a. Questions requiring *recall* ask the children about past experiences, observations, or feelings. (*Have you ever seen movies or TV programs about grizzlies?*)

    b. *Process* questions help the children to discover relationships by asking them to compare, classify, infer, or explain. (*Do you have to eat every day? Does the grizzly? Why or why not?*)

    c. *Application* questions ask children to use new information in a hypothetical situation by evaluating, imagining, or predicting.

At Home

The above aids can be used if your child is reading independently or aloud. Children will also enjoy hearing this story read aloud to them. You may want to use some of the questioning suggestions above. The story may provoke many questions from your child. Stop and answer the questions. Replying with an honest, "I don't know," provides a wonderful opportunity to head for the library to do some research together!

Have a wonderful time in your shared quest of discovery learning!

Carol A. Amato
Language-Learning Specialist